Raccoon on the moon
and other tales

Russell Punter & Lesley Sims

Illustrated by David Semple

Contents

About phonics

Phonics is a method of teaching reading used extensively in today's schools. At its heart is an emphasis on identifying the *sounds* of letters, or combinations of letters, that are then put together to make words. These sounds are known as phonemes.

Starting to read

Learning to read is an important milestone for any child. The process can begin well before children start to learn letters and put them together to read words. The sooner children can discover books and enjoy stories and language, the better they will be prepared for reading themselves, first with the help of an adult and then independently.

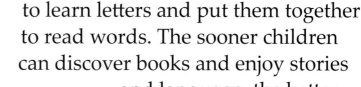

You can find out more about phonics on the Usborne Very First Reading website, **www.veryfirstreading.com**. Click on the **Parents** tab at the top of the page, then scroll down and click on **About phonics**.

Phonemic awareness

An important early stage in pre-reading and early reading is developing phonemic awareness: that is, listening out for the sounds within words. Rhymes, rhyming stories and alliteration are excellent ways of encouraging phonemic awareness.

In the following stories, your child will soon identify common sounds, such as the *ll* as in **call**; the *oa* as in **goat**; the *oo* as in **moon**; the *u* as in **bug**; the *oo* as in **zoo** and the *o (o-e)* as in **m<u>o</u>le**. Each story has lots of fun rhymes to look out for, and there are puzzles at the end of the book for further practice.

Hearing your child read

If your child is reading to you, don't rush to correct mistakes, but be ready to prompt or guide if he or she is struggling. Above all, give plenty of praise and encouragement.

Llamas in pajamas

Sam, Ali and Charlie
all yell with delight.

Please come to my
sleepover.

Frankie

There's a creepy sleepover
at Frankie's tonight.

They pick out pajamas
with stripes...

spots...

and dots.

With their packs on their backs,
off to Frankie's they trot.

Into Frankie's big bedroom
run three jolly llamas.

"Hi guys!" shouts Frankie.
"Check out my pajamas!"

Sam's pair is frilly.

Ali's are new.

Jim Jam Store

Charlie's look silly.

And Frankie's are blue.

They play games by flashlight.

"Woo-hoo!" Frankie wails.

"Let's stay up till midnight,
and tell spooky tales."

and quivering monsters,

until it's so late...

...they fall fast asleep,

but wake with a jump.

"Take cover!" calls Frankie.
"Or he'll eat us all."

BUMP! BUMP!
CLUNK! CLANK!

He's outside the door!

They hide under blankets
and slide to the floor.

CREAK! goes the door.
It opens a crack.

In creeps...

...Frankie's grandma
with a great midnight snack.

Goat in a boat

Goat eats oats.

They all eat oats...

31

"If I hook a fish, or two...

Cook can cook a fishy stew."

"I'll go for a row with Stoat," thinks Goat.

Stoat's room is bare.
There's no one there.

"Oh look! He wrote a note," says Goat.

Gone for walk.
Can't talk –
bad throat.

Stoat

Goat rows his boat around the moat.

He sits and gazes
at his float.

It sinks. He blinks.
"A fish!" he thinks.

He lifts his rod...

That's odd. It clinks.

Then Goat
spots Stoat.

Hop in
the boat!

They hear a noise among the trees.
Is it the breeze? The scared friends freeze.

An army!
Stoat has shaking knees.

The soldiers march.

Left! Right!
Left! Right!

"Shout HELP," yells Goat,
"with all your might."

But poor Stoat has a sore, sore throat.
He can't shout out along with Goat.

The castle soldiers do not hear.

Then Goat hits on a clever plan.
They bash his catch...

CLASH! CLATTER! CLANG!

The lookout hears. He gives a cry.
The drawbridge rises to the sky.

The army
can't get in.
They flee.

Goat and Stoat
row home for tea.

Goat sighs. "I have no fish for Cook."

"You do," croaks Stoat.
"Just take a look!"

Raccoon on the moon

"Goodbye!" cries Raccoon.
"I'm off to the moon.

I'll be back by lunchtime,
or late afternoon."

Goose grins and she giggles.

You foolish Raccoon!

3, 2, 1...

BOOM!

He zooms into space.

Far up to the stars,
at a fabulous pace.

He reaches the moon.
But SMASH! What a shock.

His craft crashes BUMP
on a sharp lump of rock.

The ship hits the ground.
It's split down one side.

Now I might be stuck here.

Raccoon bounds outside...

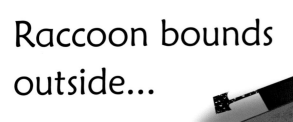

"My name is Zack. I live on the moon.

Give me your hand and
I'll have you back soon."

"Thanks," pants Raccoon.
He shows Zack his ship.

I had a bad landing.

61

Zip's buggy chugs up.

He whips out a tool.

Fizz! goes his gizmo.

The ship is fixed.

63

Let's show you around.

They bound by a crater...

64

climb mountains...

see valleys...

until, three
hours later...

The ship
reaches Earth.

"Three cheers for Raccoon!"

His chums greet their hero.

You've been to the moon!

Bug in a rug

"I need my sleep tonight,"
says Bug.

"Tomorrow I start work for Slug."

Bug glugs hot
chocolate from
a mug.

Then snuggles
up inside
his rug.

Bug hugs his bear.
He starts to nap.

Then he hears barking...

Loud party music
shakes the wall.

Below, a baby starts to bawl.

Bug plugs his ears,

but all too soon...

Owl is hooting
at the moon.

T-wit t-woo!

A car alarm adds to the row.

He plods to work at Slug's Rug Store.

"I feel so sleepy now," thinks Bug.

"And all these rugs look soft and snug..."

When Slug comes back
at ten o'clock...

...his store is packed. It's quite a shock.

Kangaroo at the zoo

And she bounces and springs

all

over

the

zoo.

A scared little monkey
leaps up a tree...

...and cries, "I'm too high!
Please, please HELP ME!"

His mother sighs. She starts to frown.
Elephant tries to lift
him down.

107

But nothing works.
Then, "Let me try!"

Kanga bounces to the sky...

Again she jumps...

and bumps
the tree.

The baby monkey falls down.

Wheeeeeee!

But Monkey lands in Kanga's pouch.

Mole in a hole

Mole gives a groan.
His home is too small.

There's no room for me! Oh... no room at all.

"I'm not very tall,
but I need a new place...

...with trees and a view
and plenty of space."

He picks up his shovel
and sticks on his hat.

"Hey!" Rabbit hops up.
"Stop, stop!"
Rabbit shouts.

"You're digging my carrots.
They're all popping out!"

Mole tries a new hole.
He finds acorns galore.

"Not there!" Squirrel squeaks.
"That's my secret store."

Mole tries a third time
near a hill, by three trees.

He sighs.
"All this digging is hard on my knees!"

I need a digger to make this hole bigger!

He digs up
old bowls,

boots
and roots,

sticks and
stones...

128

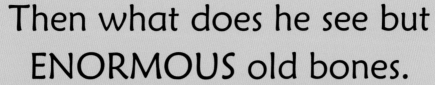

Then what does he see but
ENORMOUS old bones.

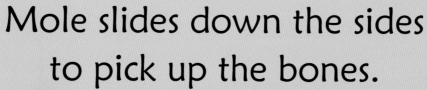

Mole slides down the sides
to pick up the bones.

What bad luck!
Mole is stuck.

He moans and
he groans.

131

He hooks them together

one bone...

two bones...

three...

Hooray! Mole is out. "Just look at the mess," shout Rabbit and Squirrel.

But how? Can you guess?

Mole works
away until it
gets dark...

Now everyone plays in

Mole's Dinosaur Park!

Puzzles

Puzzle 1

Can you find the words that rhyme?

goat	bones	bug
mug	who	groans
zoo	rug	stoat
stones	boat	moo

Puzzle 2

One word is wrong in this speech bubble.
What should it say?

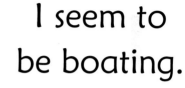

I seem to be boating.

Puzzle 3

Can you find these things in the picture?

moon   owl   dog

cat   cars

Puzzle 4

One word in each sentence is missing.
Can you say which word goes where?

| Kanga's | moon | bigger | hide |

1. They ---- under blankets.

2. I live on the ----.

3. Monkey lands in ------- pouch.

4. I need a digger to make this hole ------.

Puzzle 5

Choose the right speech bubble for each picture.

Answers to puzzles

Puzzle 1

goat   ⟶   boat   ⟶   stoat

mug   ⟶   rug   ⟶   bug

zoo   ⟶   who   ⟶   moo

stones   ⟶   bones   ⟶   groans

Puzzle 2

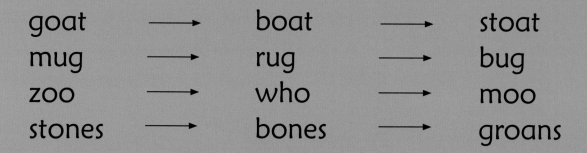

I seem to be <u>floating</u>.

Puzzle 3

moon

cat

owl

cars

dog

Puzzle 4

1. They <u>hide</u> under blankets.

2. I live on the <u>moon</u>.

3. Monkey lands in <u>Kanga's</u> pouch.

4. I need a digger to make this hole <u>bigger</u>.

Puzzle 5

He's outside the door!

Hop in the boat!

Edited by Jenny Tyler and Lesley Sims
Designed by Sam Whibley

Reading consultants: Alison Kelly and Anne Washtell